FOR MY CHILDREN ERIC, EZEQUIEL AND
ENZO, WHO ARE EVERYTHING TO ME.
- SILVIO

FOR CAROLE.
- FLAVIO

FIRST PUBLISHED IN AUSTRALIA AND NEW ZEALAND IN 2009 BY
WILKINS FARAGO PTY LTD, PO BOX 78, ALBERT PARK, VICTORIA 3206, AUSTRALIA

TEACHER'S NOTES AND OTHER DOWNLOADS: www.wilkinsfarago.com.au

© ORIGINAL EDITION: KALANDRAKA EDICIONES ANDALUCÍA, 2007
© TEXT: SILVIO FREYTES, 2007
© ILLUSTRATIONS: FLAVIO MORRIS, 2007
© ENGLISH TRANSLATION: WILKINS FARAGO PTY LTD, 2009

THE PUBLISHER WOULD LIKE TO THANK MOSES ITEN FOR HIS ASSISTANCE WITH THE ENGLISH
TRANSLATION.

NATIONAL LIBRARY OF AUSTRALIA CATALOGUING-IN-PUBLICATION ENTRY:
AUTHOR: FREYTES, SILVIO.
TITLE: IN JUST ONE SECOND / SILVIO FREYTES ; ILLUSTRATOR, FLAVIO MORRIS.
ISBN: 9780980416596 (HBK.)
TARGET AUDIENCE: FOR PRIMARY SCHOOL AGE.
SUBJECTS: TIME--JUVENILE FICTION.
OTHER AUTHORS/CONTRIBUTORS: MORRIS, FLAVIO.
DEWEY NUMBER: 863.7

PRINTED IN CHINA BY EVERBEST PRINTING
DISTRIBUTED BY TOWER BOOKS (AUSTRALIA), ADDENDA PUBLISHING (NEW ZEALAND) AND
MARKETASIA DISTRIBUTORS (SINGAPORE)

SILVIO FREYTES

IN JUST ONE SECOND

FLAVIO MORAIS

WILKINSfarago

LATE ONE AUTUMN AFTERNOON,

SOMEWHERE IN THE SOUTH OF THE CITY,

AT 27 MINUTES AND 32 SECONDS PAST SEVEN O'CLOCK,

A WOMAN DRESSED IN YELLOW

WATCHED IN GREAT SURPRISE

AS A GIRL LEANED OUT OF THE WINDOW

OF THE BUILDING IN FRONT OF HER.

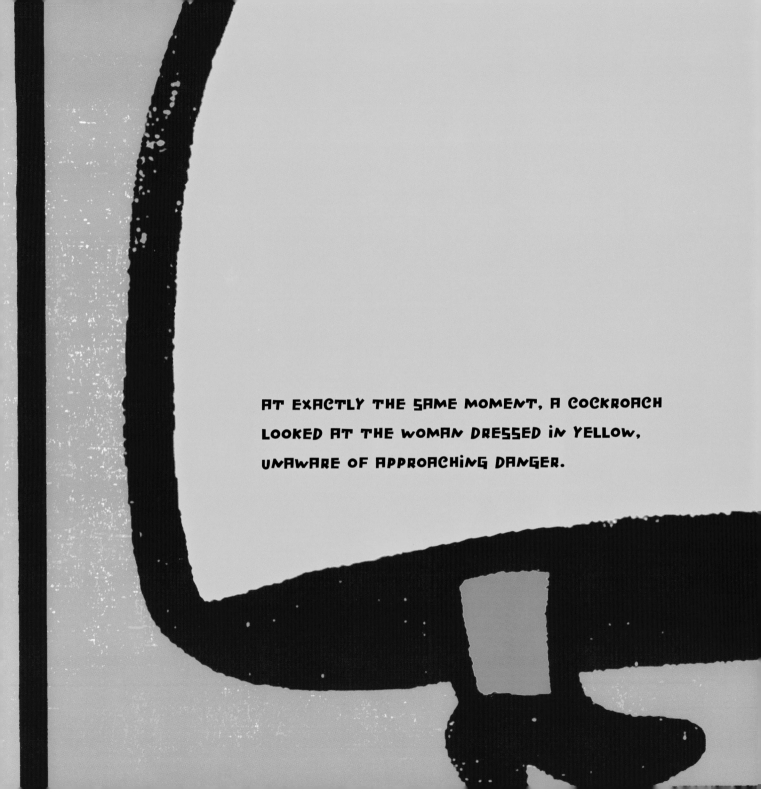

AT EXACTLY THE SAME MOMENT, A COCKROACH LOOKED AT THE WOMAN DRESSED IN YELLOW, UNAWARE OF APPROACHING DANGER.

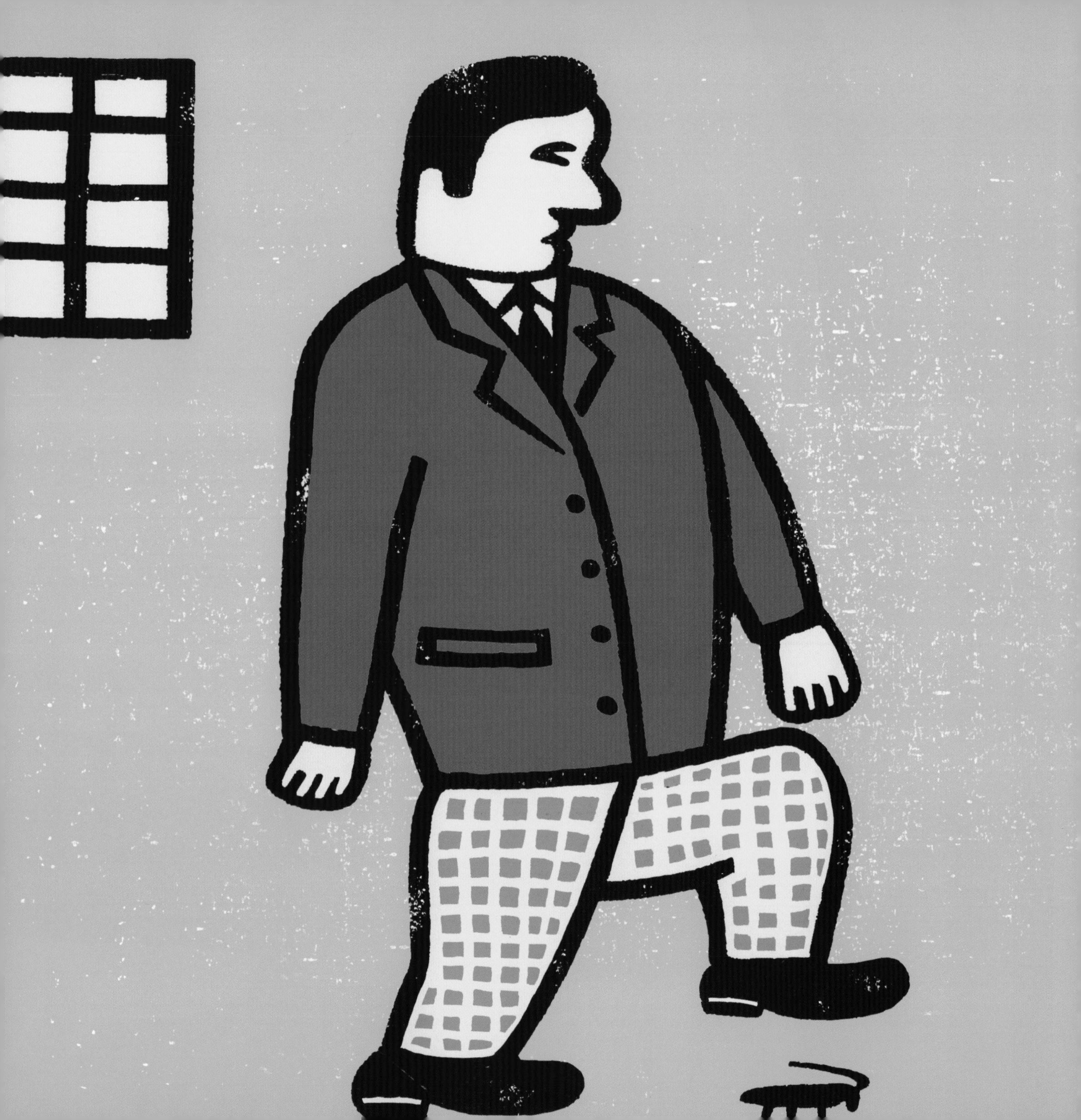

BEHIND IT, A MAN
(THE HUSBAND OF THE
WOMAN DRESSED IN
YELLOW) LIFTED A
THREATENING SHOE,
READY TO FLATTEN
THE UNSUSPECTING COCKROACH.

A BABY WATCHED THE MAN WITH HIS
SHOE IN THE AIR WITH GREAT CURIOSITY,
WONDERING WHAT HE WAS GOING TO DO NEXT.

A PLAYFUL DOG, A RUBBER BALL TRAPPED IN HIS MOUTH,
LOOKED AT THE BABY, WANTING TO CONTINUE THEIR INTERRUPTED GAME.

SAFE AND SOUND BEHIND THE WINDOW,
A CAT KEPT A WATCHFUL EYE ON THE DOG,

ANOTHER DOG, A STRAY BORN AND RAISED ON THE STREETS, EAGERLY WAITED FOR THE CAT TO CLIMB DOWN SO HE COULD CHASE IT.
HE DIDN'T REALLY KNOW WHY.

A FEW METRES AWAY, THE MAN FROM THE COUNCIL
DOG POUND SLOWLY SNEAKED UP ON THE STRAY DOG.

A PROWLING THIEF SAW THE DOG CATCHER
AND MISTOOK HIM FOR A POLICEMAN.

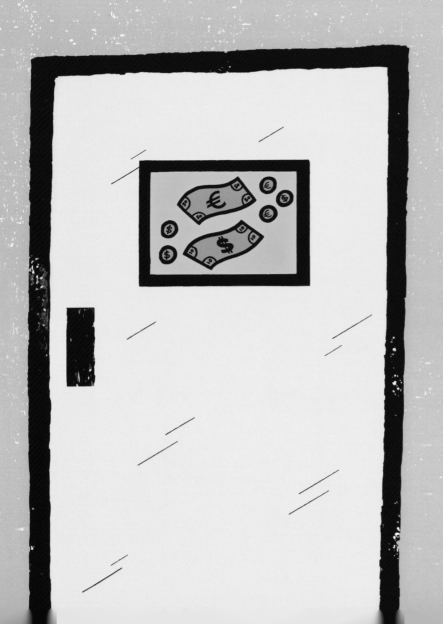

A WOMAN WAS SHOCKED TO SEE THE THIEF
AS SHE WAS TALKING ON THE TELEPHONE.

NEARBY, A PRETTY YOUNG HAIRDRESSER RECOGNISED THE WOMAN
ON THE THIRD FLOOR AS AN OLD CUSTOMER
AND WONDERED WHO SHE WAS TALKING TO.

LOST IN THOUGHT, A HANDSOME MAN LOOKED AT THE YOUNG HAIRDRESSER FROM HIS NEW CAR.

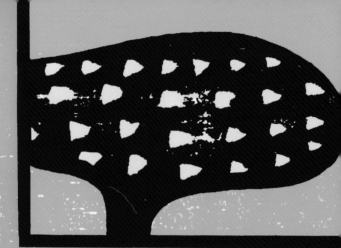

AT THAT VERY MOMENT, A MAN DRESSED AS SANTA CLAUS
REALISED THAT THE DRIVER OF THE CAR
WAS AN OLD FRIEND HE HADN'T SEEN
FOR MORE THAN 25 YEARS.

MEANWHILE, THE GIRL HANGING OUT OF THE WINDOW
SAW SANTA CLAUS.

ALL THIS HAPPENED LATE ONE AUTUMN AFTERNOON,
SOMEWHERE IN THE SOUTH OF THE CITY.

EVERYONE WAS SO BUSY LOOKING AT OTHER PEOPLE,
THEY DIDN'T NOTICE WHO WAS LOOKING AT THEM.

IT WAS EXACTLY 27 MINUTES AND 32 SECONDS
PAST SEVEN O'CLOCK.

IT ALL HAPPENED IN JUST ONE SECOND.